Statistics

A Short Story

Hayley Pegg

PublishAmerica
Baltimore

First printing

ISBN: 1-4241-0010-0
PUBLISHED BY
PUBLISHAMERICA, LLLP.
www.publishamerica.com
Baltimore

Printed in the United States of America

To the one and only Ginger, you beauty.

Acknowledgements

Many thanks to my wonderful family who mean the world to me. To my friends, especially Anna Wood and Sarah Pitt. A huge thank you to PublishAmerica for making a dream come true. To all my fellow students and staff at the Ursuline, and, lastly, to all, both sides of The Green Man Pub for help with my "character building." May an angel always be by your sides!

Chapter 1

AS LOUISE STUMBLED AWAY FROM THE pure, closed, white with innocence bedroom door, she felt the piercing pain build up in her eyes. The words she heard haunted her all night as she cried herself to sleep. She suddenly felt insecure and not safe; she felt betrayed.

"I hate you. I don't love you. I don't want to be with you! It can't work, not even for the children. It's over...."

Those were the words of her parents, Ian and Jill, who had been happily married—or so Louise was led to believe—for 20 years. Of course they argued, but all parents argued. However, Louise didn't want them to become divorced. Her best friend's parents divorced when she was young and Louise had seen how hard this was for her. Although her mum remarried, her hatred for her dad still remained and Louise couldn't deal with that if it happened.

In the year after that night Louise concentrated all her thinking time on her school work and exams, she hardly was ever at home and made constant commitments to sports and events to forget the words of hatred that had come out of her guardians' mouths.

Seven years on and Louise still hadn't one hundred percent got used to the idea that her own mother and father were separated. After work she would go home, get changed and go running. Running had always made her relax, she would run for miles unaware of anything around her and every day the same thought would circle around her mind.

How could it happen to the Adams family? The Adams family who had a successful banker as the father, a secretary as a mother, a fifteen-year-old daughter called Vicky who was to be the next big thing in the theatre world, another daughter who was Louise who was quieter than Vicky but a down-to-earth girl. Then there was the seventeen-year-old son who attended college and was to become the next David Beckham.

This was the Adams family who was accompanied by Molly the Cat. This was the Adams family who became a statistic when her parents got divorced, a statistic when her father was diagnosed with cancer two years before!

Louise also remembered that event very well, that was why the divorce had come as a shock.

The family had just come back from a holiday and Ian had to go to the hospital to re x-ray his arm as he broke it while skiing. While at the hospital the doctor gave him a full check-up and took some blood. It was later when the doctor told of the news of his condition, which was the first stage of cancer.

Louise remembered it like yesterday, when her dad told her. Her automatic response was to cry. He reassured her everything would be OK. However, she couldn't help the tears from falling. Her sister Vicky asked if he would still be able to fix her hair irons—that was just like Vicky, although she was a lovely girl, there was no denying that she was materialistic. Luke took it well but chose not to talk about it. Jill was absolutely devastated.

After the operation, etc., the year flew by. Ian recovered quickly and was back to his normal self and the family was how it used to be until Louise found herself torn between her mother and father. The statistic about divorce was set in the Adams family but hopefully not in Louise's life!

Chapter 2

LOUISE ENJOYED HER TRAINING AT MAX Williams; she had taken law for A-level and succeeded in it so she decided that was the career for her. Although she was twenty-four, she hadn't really been in any serious relationships. She felt it hard to trust anyone since the people who meant the most to her betrayed her.

James was also twenty-four and was training at Max Williams; he hoped that he could be the one she would trust. He really fancied Louise; the physical attraction of her long blonde hair, brown eyes, tall lean figure and a pair of fantastic legs. Whenever Louise would walk past James it would wake him up, but it wasn't the legs that attracted him so much it was the brown eyes that was so attractive and the mind behind them. There was mystery present in her eyes and if only he knew what was making her sad or even hurt, the heaviness in her eyes may disappear.

For the meantime, this was what distanced her away from the rest of the girls. Of course you had the office slut Jackie, who everyone knew she only got where she was today by sleeping with the boss Mike, then his brother Dave. She was too easy for James;

he wanted a challenge. There were other girls in the office: Jane, Debbie, Sarah and Kate, who all had the same physical attributes as Louise but they all lacked the mystery present in the eyes.

James and Louise talked regularly but it was all work related, Louise was very conscious and whenever the discussion turned to personal, she made her excuses and hurried away. She also had this nervous habit of fiddling with her hair that James also found irresistible.

Louise was too busy with her work to notice James but if she did she would notice his mousy brown hair that flopped down into his ice blue eyes, his soft lips which led to a lean tall body. She would notice a man who dressed to impress and who was begging to get to know her better.

It was 9 a.m. Monday morning and Louise was already in the office. Looking around at the empty offices, she felt relaxed and calm, it felt strange she could hear the birds and…

"Ring, ring, ring…."

"Louise Adams, Max Williams. Good morning, eh, I mean, Max Williams, Louise speaking…."

"Hello, hi, dear, haven't heard from you in a while."

"Hi, Mum."

"I rang to see if you are OK."

"Yeah, I fine. Thanks, Mum."

"Good. Well, I am inviting you to a summer party and, Louise, it would be nice if you would bring someone."

"Is Dad going to be there?"

"Yes, yes, dear. You are always worrying about your father. He will be there. So who are you going to bring?"

"I don't know if I'm going yet. When is it?"

"Next Saturday."

"Oh, well…."

"*Louise*, you never come."

"What time?"

"One o clock."

"OK. I'll be there."

"Good and your brother and sister are coming to, who are you bringing?"

Louise was looking at a memo when James walked into the office carrying his morning coffee and a croissant in the other hand. "James."

"Oh, who's James?"

"No, Mum, I didn't mean I was bringing…"

"OK, dear, must dash I'll see you and your mystery James on Saturday."

And she hung up.

Louise felt embarrassed. How could she turn up arm empty yet again? Every time she saw her sister or brother they had someone new and she had no one!

"Hi, James. I was just reading this memo about the hearing nine o'clock Saturday, you and I are down to attend but if you have other arrangements with your family or girlfriend, don't worry."

Oh, my God, why did I just say that!

Louise started to blush. James didn't speak; his ice blue eyes met hers, he gave her a wink and said there was no girlfriend, and he strolled off.

Louise didn't know why but she felt relieved that he didn't have a girlfriend. She felt sick and had pins and needles in her arm. What was she thinking? She had to get a grip.

She looked up from her desk and saw the ice blue eyes stare at her; her heart melted.

Chapter 3

"JAMES."

"Oh, hi, Jackie, how can I help?" *God, what does she want?* he thought. *She is in my way. I can't see Louise.*

"I was just wondering—well, not only me, the whole group of girls—Jane, Debbie, Sarah and Kate—were thinking that we should go for a summer drink."

"Yeah sounds good, when?"

"Tonight."

"Tonight?"

"Yeah tonight. It's a lovely day and it will be a lovely evening and anyway you look like you need a drink."

Cheers, James thought, *only because you look like you're the cat who got the cream.*

"OK. I'll email you the venue."

"OK."

And she turned around, bent over so her suspenders were on show and waltz off.

Louise saw all of this. She was distracted by the high-pitched tone coming out of Jackie's mouth. She couldn't hear what they were saying but what she did know James was obviously not the type of guy she thought. She thought he was decent and he had taste. Obviously not if he was chatting up Jackie.

Not soon after James stopped talking to Jackie and went to get a coffee, a new email appeared on his screen.

From: Jackie
To: James
Subject: A drink!

7 o'clock
The Havelock
X

That was all he needed; all the girls and him. What a great Monday night this was going to turn out to be.

When James first saw the advert for the position at Max Williams, it seemed the perfect place; he needed a placement quickly and soon applied.

When he arrived at the building for his interview, he was intrigued to find out that it was an all women's department he would be working in. Although around the building there were men, not one of them worked in the criminal department.

The interview was a breeze and on 8 August he and this lady called Louise started training. James couldn't believe how much this girl had interested him; he needed to speak to her outside the building, but when? And how?

He didn't know why but he sent her an email.

From: James
To: Louise
Subject: Department drink

All to attend
7 o'clock
The Havelock

James
X

Louise was interrupted by a blinking message about a new email. When she opened it, she felt butterflies in her stomach as she read James's name. She didn't really fancy an evening with the girls; however, she wouldn't mind an evening or even a morning with James!

Now that would be something...

Chapter 4

TWO COURT CASES AND FIFTEEN BRIEF takings later, Louise found herself sat at a table with four women and one man, four vodkas and oranges and two dry white wines.

It was funny, Louise had always imagined James to be a straight vodka or martini guy, but he liked the same as Louise.

Louise wasn't fussed what wine James got and would be happy with the house; however, he chose the most expensive one on the list. The conversation was as dry as the wine and all Louise could concentrate on was the skirt of Jackie's riding up her thigh every thirty seconds. James chose to ignore and was talking about work. Louise had wondered why this drink meeting was so urgent.

The evening dragged on and so far the only interesting information Louise retrieved from the conversation was that Sarah and Kate had been with their boyfriends for two years on and off. Jane was a feminist and Debbie was into the younger model as she put it.

So it was only Jackie. Although she was six years older than James, she still thought she had a chance with him. The talk was becoming tedious and Jackie was making a show of herself. James was obviously not interested but she couldn't see that. The younger girls disappeared and it was just the love triangle left, Louise thought. No, what was she thinking? She meant the trio was left. That was three people. Her, James and Jackie, the same as a triangle. Louise downed her glass so her thought would disappear.

Jackie was all over James like a hot rash. It was ten minutes to midnight and Louise could only think about the early start tomorrow. So when James said he would call a taxi, the relief was present on Louise's face.

Jackie refused to come, she was more interested or should we say involved with the group of men attached to her inch-long skirt.

James and Louise stepped out of the pub; the fresh air rushed into Louise's lungs and made her gasp.

"You OK?"

"Yes, thank you." She noticed she was shivering and so did James. He slid his pinstriped jacket off and placed it gently on her shoulders.

"Thanks."

"No worries." Louise could feel her heart melt again as she caught his ice blue eyes.

They stared at each other for a while not saying anything just reading each other's eyes.

What makes those deep eyes so mysterious? I want to know, James thought.

I wish he wouldn't stare at me with those puppy dog eyes, Louise thought.

James broke off the eye contact first; it was as though he had really read her mind.

A taxi stopped in front of them, they decided to share it. The warmth of James's jacket was confronting to Louise and James could sense it. The taxi driver was the chatty type. He was talking about how busy he had been. James was being polite and listened. The driver then began to ask questions. Louise wasn't interested until the driver asked James, "So how long you two been together? I must say you're lucky, mate, to get a catch like that."

Louise could feel herself blush; James didn't notice and informed the driver that they were not a couple. The driver seemed in disbelief. "But you make a perfect couple."

James looked at Louise and winked, she winked back and James moved closer. He touched her hand, and ran his fingers up her arm and moved in for the kiss....

Chapter 5

THE KISS OR SO IT WOULD have been was interrupted by the taxi driver shouting: "4 Hawkings Drive!" Louise's address. She jumped out, told James she would see him tomorrow and sprinted to the front door. She rushed through the door and collapsed onto the sofa. Her heart was in overdrive. It was only when she had calmed down that she noticed she still had his jacket; she placed it over the back of the sofa, unravelled herself out of her clothes and flopped into bed.

Constant knocking on her front door and her dog licking her feet was what finally made Louise give in to getting up.

She rolled out of bed only in her underwear, grabbing the first jacket she could find and answered the door.

She could have cried when she opened the door and saw the familiar ice blue eyes staring down at her. "Suits you." He smiled.

She realised the pinstriped jacket was clinging onto her. She blushed slightly and quickly took the jacket off, only to feel once again like she could have cried, when remembering she was only in her underwear. James gave her a quick glance and handed her back the jacket.

"It looks better on you anyway."

She made her excuses and went into the bathroom.

The smirk was still on James's face when Louise left him to "make himself at home."

He was confronted by Sophie the Labrador. He sat comfortable on the cream sofa and waited for Louise.

It was 8:10 and James was starving. He went to the kitchen and was faced with a fruit bowl, a cupboard full of cereal bars, croissants pasta and beverages.

No wonder she keeps herself fit and healthy, James thought and there was more evidence. Her calendar was full of gym and running appointments and some parties including a summer party which was dated for today.

James fixed up coffee and croissants and sat down. Still accompanied by the dog, he looked over the notes.

Meanwhile Louise was panicking. "I don't believe he saw me in my underwear." That was all she could say. She pulled apart her wardrobe and found a white pinstriped suit. When she was groomed to perfection, she joined James in the kitchen. He greeted her with breakfast which Louise accepted gratefully.

Louise started the conversation. "I would just like to apologise for earlier, I don't make it a habit of walking around in my underwear."

"Oh, don't you? That's a shame!"

Louise giggled. She couldn't believe how down to earth and cheeky this guy was.

During the next hour they managed to get all the notes completed and four cups of coffee digested. The conversation quickly turned into personal and for the first time in seven years, Louise felt comfortable in talking about her past.

However, she didn't talk about her past first of all; she managed to tell him she had a brother who trained at Charlton Athletic and a sister who was working in the theatre.

She found out that he had a sister a year younger and she was a vet.

After only telling him that she realised she had a summer party today, she had to invite him, but how?

"Eh, James, I was just wondering...my mother has organised a summer party today and I was just wondering, if you wanted we could finish off our notes at hers?"

"But we have finished the notes."

"Oh, yeah, I forgot, erm, do you fancy a drink...it doesn't matter, don't worry."

"No, I mean I would love to go with you as your, your friend. It's a date!"

Chapter 6

IT WAS 11:30. JAMES OFFERED TO take Sophie out for a walk and meet Louise back at her place at 12:00. Louise had half an hour to get ready, and she had already spent half an hour watching James and Sophie in the park. The laughter on his face as he ran and jumped with Sophie was amazing; so much energy. Sophie took to James straight away which secured Louise's thoughts.

Louise washed her hair and tried something new; she curled her hair into ringlets, loose and free. It was a different style and one Louise liked. It was different to the straight long hair; she wondered what made her try something different with her hair. It probably came down to seeing her sister at the party and always admiring her different hairstyles.

She decided to wear a tropical green three-quarter length dress; it hung nicely on her figure and when she answered the door to a dashing James, she could see his mouth drop.

"My God, you look gorgeous."

"Thank you."

He leaned forward and gave her a kiss on the cheek; it felt so natural and right. The tension in Louise's shoulders relaxed.

Sophie was left asleep by the fire and James and Louise set off to Kent where her mother's house was.

There was much more to Louise than what you saw was what you got and James knew this. He didn't want to pressure her by asking twenty-one questions, so he asked about her bringing up, school, hobbies—the normal questions you ask, well that was if there were any such thing as normal questions.

They found out they both liked tennis and reading. They both had the same views on political relations which had made a heated conversation. They both enjoyed drama series, and both had their views about Jackie at work!

While Louise was talking away, it suddenly hit her that she hadn't told James that her parents were divorced. Her smile faded. She panicked. What was she to do? What would he think? Louise knew what he would think; he would think she was from an unstable family, that her father had affairs or her mother was too high maintenance. He would think because of how her parents were, she must be the same. James would think that her brother and sister were out of control and had serious depression or even she had issues which she would only discuss with a psychologist.

This was not the case. Although Louise hadn't yet come to terms with the divorce, she didn't visit psychologist or break down into serious depression. She realised that, that was the easy way out and she had to carry on with her life!

Louise couldn't face having her personality and her image stereotyped and misjudged because of her parents. As it turned out neither her mother nor father was having affairs or were high maintenance, but Louise had seen it all before. Questions started flying, rumours, judgements were made and she didn't want James to make the judgements.

In all of this panicking, what Louise failed to realise was that everyone judged everyone else. That was part of being human and was an automatic thought, consciously or subconsciously. She was judging James; she hadn't even got to know him well yet she was judging him on how he would judge her family.

Didn't that make her a statistic?

Chapter 7

AS THE BLACK FORD FOCUS PULLED into the drive of her mother's manor house, Louise's smile had not yet reappeared. She could feel her breathing quicken. For the rest of the journey, she had been making plan after plan after back-up plans of how she was to fool or mislead James into believing her parents were still together.

They walked up to the house and James gave Louise a tight squeeze. He could see she was nervous and didn't know what to expect. The loud shouts from her mother were the first thing Louise noticed. She came rushing up to them, greeting Louise and then turning to James. She herself couldn't resist the ice blue eyes and all Louise could think was: *Mother, leave off, he's mine.*

"Mrs Adams, nice to meet you."

"You may call me Jill. Would you like a drink with blue ice? I mean ice?"

James couldn't help but giggle although Louise didn't look too impressed. Jill or Mrs Adams asked thirty-two questions in a row. Obviously Louise didn't take after her mother!

"So, James, my last question is, are you looking after my little girl?"

"Mother, stop it. Me and James are well…erm."

"Mrs Adams, or may I call you Jill?"

"Yes, of course."

"I assure you I am looking after your little girl," he said and gave her a wink.

Louise knew bringing James to the party was a bad idea; she walked over to the punch bowl and helped herself to two large glasses.

Jill's heart melted. She was so happy for her little girl. James was charming. If she were thirty years younger, she would definitely go for him. Those eyes were so magical! She stared at both of them from across the room and prayed to God that this was the one for Louise.

"Your mother is pleasant. A really nice person. She obviously cares about you."

"Yeah. Sorry about all the questions. When she starts, it's hard for her to stop."

"That's OK. You should meet my mother. You wouldn't get a word in edgeways."

Louise giggled. She started to relax until she saw her sister and brother approach her. She felt an inch tall. They were both smaller than Louise but she felt below them when they talked to her. Of course they both brought someone. Vicky was arm in arm with what could only be described as a man of the theatre! If Louise didn't know better, she would have said he was gay, and Luke was accompanied by an elegant bean pole.

Louise was too sacred to shake or even greet the girl just in case she fell into two.

"Hello, sis, long time no see!"

"Hi, Vicks. How is the theatre? Did you get my research?"

"Sshh, Louise. He thinks I did all of that myself, but yeah thanks. I owe you one."

James knew that Vicky took advantage of her sister, and she was only where she was today by her sister giving her an extra push.

Louise didn't except Vicky to repay her. "I owe you one" had been said to her so many times in the past that it went in one ear and out the other.

"Hi, sis, you look fab."

"Thanks, so do you."

Luke didn't take so much of an advantage out of Louise; however, on occasions Louise had helped him out; he was more realistic compared to Vicky.

Not in the sense that they were both living, more in the way that Vicky could be a real selfish bitch sometimes and all she cared about was herself and her status in life, whereas Luke cared about his status but would always be there if Louise needed to talk; it had always been like that and Louise felt it would never change.

"Have you seen Dad? He looks terrible. I think he is really struggling with the—"

"Weather, it's terrible, isn't it? Hay fever? Mine's not to bad."

Luke looked at Louise. Was she feeling OK? "No, I mean I think he is finding it really hard—"

"In the sun. He's got very pale skin. Quite funny, you should see him when he gets burnt." Louise started hysterically laughing.

"You OK, Louise? You seem a bit funny."

"Yeah, I'm fine. I might go and check on Dad. Catch you later."

"Nice to meet you, James. Hopefully we will meet again."

Louise went to get another drink, Vicky was standing there. "Is Dad OK?"

"I think so. I haven't seen him yet. Me and Luke are worried. Mum's found a new partner."

"In her business. How nice for her. I must congratulate her when I see her."

"Her business? What are you on about, Louise?"

Louise walked off and left James talking to her sister, the theatre man, whose name was Wayne, was entertaining the cousins. Louise could see her dad in the corner. She ran over to him and gave him a hug.

"Hello, sweetie, how are you? You look great. You look like you've lost weight. You really should eat more, Louise. I still want to be there at your wedding!"

"I'm OK. Thanks, Dad. How are you?"

"You know, every day is a new day. I'm getting there, love."

James walked over to Louise. Louise introduced James. James could see that Louise took after her father straightaway; the figure, the hair, the height and the eyes—they had the same eyes….

Chapter 8

"SMILE; IT CONFUSES PEOPLE," THAT'S WHAT Ian had said when talking to James and Louise, and he was right. "People wonder why you are smiling," he said. "When they know what your past is and all you do is smile, they think you're hiding something. It's great."

"Sorry, Ian, I don't understand."

"Oh, sorry, hasn't Louise told you?"

"Told me what?" James looked at Louise. She lowered her head and made her excuse to go to the ladies.

Ian told James everything and for the next hour, they talked. Ian told all about Louise so James could get to know her better.

Meanwhile Louise revisited her childhood bedroom. It was still exactly how she had left it four years ago. She sat on her bed and looked through the photo album on the side. So many memories lay before her of school, her friends, her family and Louise knew that the life she was living was partly what she was making it and partly what was made by the friends whom she chose. That was why her friends were who they were. That was why she was who she was.

The memories that flicked past her were too much for her to deal with and she felt seven years of tears pouring from her eyes.

Louise now had to leave the past behind, so she wrapped the photo album up and placed it in her bottom draw.

She carried on sitting on her bed, and glanced at her watch; an hour since she left James, an hour since her father confessed all, an hour since James changed his attitude towards Louise. He had probably left because of the disgrace of the truth. Of course James wouldn't want to know her now, wouldn't want to speak to her or ever see her again. The warmth of Louise's tears gradually reduced her to sleep.

Downstairs, all the guests were leaving, and Louise's sister and brother had disappeared; they had sent their love to Louise, who James excused due to a headache. They both promised they would ring her soon.

Louise's mother, Jill, was in the arms of her new partner and they seemed extremely comfortable. Ian had begun a conversation with a mature lady named Holly, and they had already made plans to meet again.

All was well downstairs and James felt he should check on Louise. He had the experience and knowledge to give people space; however, he was concerned.

He tiptoed up the cream stairs and went in search for Louise. He passed an empty room which was full of posters of musicals and guessed it was Vicky's.

Then there was a bedroom full of football posters, three guesses it was Luke's. Then there was a closed white door in the corner of the house.

James turned the handle and saw a picture-perfect image before him; Louise was curled up on the bed asleep. She looked so peaceful and childlike; James pulled a duvet over the top of her, took her shoes off and placed a pillow underneath her head.

While doing so he caught her face with his hand. Her face was wet, with warm tears. He couldn't understand why she would be crying. He decided to let her sleep.

Chapter 9

LOUISE AWOKE TO THE SMELL OF freshly squeezed orange juice and warm bread.

She had stayed for breakfast, and then reassured her mother that she felt better and needed to return home for Sophie. They promised to meet for lunch in the week to discuss about Matt, her new partner....

Louise reached 4 Hawkings Drive with the aid of a taxi, as James had taken the car; she wondered what he might have said. Or even why he left.

She opened the door and was greeted by Sophie. Putting the keys on the side, she noticed a large bouquet of flowers. Her first thought was that they were from her dad.

She would always remember the little gifts her father would present to her, so little and worthless to her sister or brother but not to her; they would brighten up her day, because it was the little things in life that were important to Louise.

However the flowers, six yellow, six pink and six white roses were not from her father but from James.

The note read:

> Isn't it strange that we talk least about the things we think about the most? Here if you need to talk!
>
> James
> X

Louise held the note close to her heart. "He is right. I never talk about my father, my sister, my mother or my brother. I never talk about my parents' divorce or anything that troubles me. I always push the thoughts away; however, the thoughts are always there and I always think about them."

Louise decided to take action and talk to James, she owed him an explanation. She picked up her mobile, dialled the number, and pressed the green button.

The phone rung; however, Louise couldn't go through with it. She put the phone down and took a bath.

She filled it to the top with bubbles and piping hot water, the heat softened her muscles top to bottom and the bubbles tingled her skin. Time flew by and Louise could feel the sun on her skin as it shone through the window. Sophie was jumping up, causing the bubbles to fall on her nose.

Louise got out of the bath, pulled out a chocolate brown tracksuit and stepped out with Sophie into the late Sunday afternoon. A quick jog and Louise and Sophie found themselves outside the gates of Hyde Park.

James hadn't heard from Louise and was getting frustrated with the naivety of her. If help was being offered, why not take it?

James got up, left all the case papers spread across his wooden table and jumped into his car.

Twelve minutes later James found himself in front of the gates of Hyde Park and in search for a lady and her dog.

It didn't take James long to spot Sophie; she was exhausting Louise, who was flopped on the floor.

Sophie was left free to run and appeared next to James; he held her close to him and carried her back to the young lady laid out across the grass. His nose was soaking from the constant licking of Sophie.

Louise opened her eyes. A tall figure was blocking her sunlight. She raised her hand to her eyes and was blinded by a pair of deep blue eyes that carried a certain gift of reappearing.

Chapter 10

HE GAVE OUT HIS HAND TO help her up; the strong grip held her unstable body.

"You OK? I've been worried."

"I'm OK."

"No you're not, I can tell."

"Why are you here? I didn't think you wanted to talk to me now you know."

"Now I know what?"

Louise looked to the floor. "About my parents' divorce."

"And why would I not talk to you?"

"Because you would think I am the same as my parents, the same temperament, and had the same attitude on life."

James looked hurt. "Do you really think that?"

"I think I do. I didn't mean to judge you, but it's just the world thinks the same. I was afraid you would think I was from an unstable family and that I was depressed, etc."

"So do you think all that about me?"

Louise looked at James with confusion.

"Well, do you?"

Louise looked at James. "Do you mean that your parents, your parents are divorced?"

"Yes."

Louise sunk to the ground with her head in her hands and slightly cried. How could she have been so selfish? How could she have judged him? He had been so nice but she had already assumed what his reaction would be.

James sat down beside her, and began to retell the past, his past. He told how he couldn't take it in, how he hoped he would live within a close family, all his life with no problems or interference from anyone else in the world.

As the divorce was settled, he began to believe that all of these challenges and obstacles were put in place to make us better people. And began to lead his life.

Louise listened to James and felt an urge to give him a hug. He dared not look at her, and instead he stayed in front of him. He recalled the whole past and all he ever felt.

Suddenly his tone of voice changed. He jumped out, grabbed Sophie, turned to Louise and said, "Never look back unless you are planning to go that way," and added a wink.

Those were the words that made Louise's mind click. She had been looking back for the past fours years, she had been looking back to the night of her parents' divorce and had blamed herself.

James linked arms with Louise, led them back to his car, drove to her house. Louise had invited him in for a late dinner and he had accepted.

While Sophie lay asleep by the fire, James held Louise close on the sofa. She looked up at him still with those mysterious eyes that James had hoped would disappear after today, and softly kissed him. She continued to look at him and said, "You know something, Mr Stewart. Those eyes of yours sure do contain some important information! Seriously, James, thank you for today. What you said is the truth. It's just hard sometimes to accept the truth. I also apologise for judging you. I didn't mean to. I didn't realise your parents were divorced and I didn't mean to storm off at the party."

"Stop apologising. It's OK. I understand." Although James didn't understand why her eyes were still full of mysterious.

"Oh, and thank you for the flowers. They are beautiful. All different layers and colours."

"Just like yourself."

She giggled. He held her hand, looked at her and said, "You know something, Miss Adams, your eyes contain a hidden message which hasn't yet been told!"

Chapter 11

LOUISE HAD SLEPT PEACEFULLY; SHE DIDN'T think about the day's events and she didn't revisit conversations like she normally did. Instead her mind was blank and she had found it a struggle to rise for work.

She prepared breakfast on the go, and rushed to the office.

As she reached her desk, her phone rang. "Hello."

"Hello, dear, you OK? Lunch at twelve? One?"

"Hi, Mum. That sounds fine."

"OK, we will chat then."

"I will meet you in the lobby at twelve, bye."

Louise had always turned a blind eye to the fact that neither she nor her mother could talk on the phone. Sometimes when out shopping, Louise would hear girls talking about everything for ages to their mums. Louise envied this, because it was never like that with her mother and Louise was certain it would never be that way.

If talking was to be done, it would have to be face to face, in a letter or not at all. Somehow Louise felt comfortable with this idea. She would text her mother from time to time but they would hardly

hold a conversation on the phone.
Z friends with men!

"So, does she live near? I will have to meet her."

"Would you, Louise? That would be great. I'll arrange something and call you."

"OK, well, I'm glad you're OK. I'll have to go. I'll speak to you soon."

"Take care."

"You too."

Louise put the phone down and looked up. A quick glance and she noticed Jackie whispering to Jane, Debbie, Sarah and Kate were all working, and James, well, James was just sitting there and staring at Louise.

Louise snapped out of the stare. She realised she had just been sitting there staring at James. He walked over and smiled.

"Hi, you OK?"

"Feeling better. Yesterday was great. We will have to do that again."

Out of nowhere Jackie appeared. "What will you have to do again?"

James turned around. "I wasn't talking to you, Jackie."

Jackie glared at James and walked off.

"Yeah, we should."

"Just spoke to my dad. He says hi. He was telling me about Holy."

"Oh, yeah, she was getting on well with your dad. See, it worked out for them."

"Yeah, I know. They're lucky, aren't they? For most it never works out."

"How do you know that?"

"I don't but, I mean well, it doesn't, it can't."

"Why?"

"Because it can't, or can it?"

"You're such a pessimistic, Miss Adams. You need to look out of that bubble of yours."

He laughed and handed her a coffee. "I'll speak to you later."

Louise wasn't a pessimistic or well she hoped she wasn't. She didn't mean to turn everything into a negative; she just felt that she couldn't win in the world.

She was positive for her mum and dad and her sister and brother. She was happy that her dad was moving on and living his life. She just had to live hers.

Chapter 12

From: Jackie
To: James

I'll meet you at 7
Don't be late
Xxx

LOUISE'S HEART SANK, SHE COULD FEEL the frustration build up inside.

What was going on? James didn't like Jackie! What was she up to?

Louise had to do something. She was acting like a jealous cow. She couldn't lose to Jackie.

She thought about sending the email back and noting: "Wrong person, hope you have a good time!"

However, her same old way of thinking stopped her. Why did she have to be so much of a coward? Instead, she deleted the email, carried on with her work and acted as though she hadn't seen anything.

But she had seen something!

She had read it!

And now she felt hurt and betrayed, once again.

After a coffee, Louise found herself asking, *Maybe I was overreacting. They may just be meeting up. There's no harm in that is there?*

She looked at her watch, her mum! She rushed out of the office, down the stairs, and went in search of her mum.

Louise looked left then right, and there she was over in the corner, smartly dressed as always. Louise couldn't believe sometimes that her mum was fifty; she looked younger than her, platinum blonde hair, blue eyes, petite figure and a glowing smile. Louise took after her dad with the appearance.

As Louise got closer, she noticed her mum was sitting opposite Jackie! Louise was getting fed up with Jackie and it was only Monday.

"Hi, Mum. Hi, Jackie. Are we ready to go?"

"Oh, hi, Louise. Your mum was just telling me about Saturday. Sounds like your mum can throw a smashing party!"

"Yes, dear, I said the next party I have you will have to invite Jackie."

"Your mum was also halfway into telling me about the gorgeous man you brought with you. Who would that have been? Anyone I know?"

Jackie smirked. Of course she knew it was James. "James." Louise looked at Jackie.

"Oh, yeah, that was it, James. Louise did say he had come-to-bed eyes."

"Did you, Louise? Now that's interesting! Must hurry late for a meeting. Hopefully we will meet again, Mrs Adams!"

And that was it. Jackie had her fixed smirk on her face and waltzed up the stairs.

All Louise could think was: *Cheers, Mum!*

"She seemed nice. I haven't heard you talk about her before. You will have to invite her round, and she sounds like she can handle a party. She was strangely interested in how you and James got along."

"Was she now?"

"Sorry, dear, I missed that."

"Nothing, Mum, I was talking to myself."

Louise also admitted that her mother wasn't the best judge of character.

That was it, all the way to the café, all Louise could think was about Jackie and the look in her eyes as she heard James's name. Hopefully James wouldn't be stupid enough to fall for her!

"Are you OK, dear? You seem quiet."

"I'm OK. I spoke to Dad earlier. He sounds happy. So, how are you?"

"Me and Matt are fine."

In the next half an hour Louise had come to know everything about Matt:

> Matt Alexander Lewis
> Six foot
> 2 cats—Tiger and Sam
> Retired constable now serving as a PC
> Madly in love with Jill Adams

As Louise listened to her mother and noted down the bullet points, she released a glint in her eyes that had never been there before. She looked radiant, on a high, she didn't stop talking and she seemed the happiest Louise had seen her for years.

Louise and her mum promised to meet up next week and Matt was invited. Jill, although was buzzing about her newfound love, noticed the sadness present in her daughter's eyes. She knew there was something wrong or troubling Louise, but felt she would leave Louise to sort it.

When Louise arrived back at the office, Jackie still had the smirk on her face, and James was working hard. Louise decided to bury herself into a case, which she knew would keep her occupied till leaving time.

At six o'clock Louise looked up; the office was empty apart from Mike and Dave who were in a meeting. She closed all her files, turned her computer off and went to grab her bag.

The note attached was from James: "At Local if you fancy. A quick one!"

Sure, Louise thought, *that's just what I want to do, not!* Louise grabbed her coat, walked past the station and went to tell James she was too tired. As she reached the pub, she could hear the screech of Jackie's voice. She looked over at the table and saw James and Jackie sipping drinks. Jackie looked up, saw Louise and moved in to kiss James; Louise couldn't believe it. What a bitch! A manipulating bitch!

James pulled away. "What do you think you are doing?"

"I thought you wanted me to."

"Well, you thought wrong!"

"Suit yourself."

James pulled his coat from behind Jackie and left the pub. The outrage he felt was noticeable. *What a stupid cow*, he thought.

Louise had grabbed a taxi and stared out the window all the way back to her house. When entering the front door, she fell to the floor. *How could he?* That was all she could think!

She felt sick, she pulled herself together and changed. She left her car, looked at her watch: 10:30. She grabbed a scarf, fed the dog, and went for a walk.

She didn't know why, but she let her body lead her. She walked continuously until she stopped. She turned and faced the sign of the road: "Park Road." James's road!

What was she doing here? Why had she come? What was she to say?

She walked along the road, till she reached number nine and climbed the stairs. She would give him what for. He deserved it!

She knocked on the door and was startled when someone was at home. She saw the figure approach the door; it couldn't be James, he was at the pub!

The figure opened the door; it was James.

"Louise, what are you doing here?"

Chapter 13

"WHAT ARE YOU DOING HERE?"

"Well, funny enough, this is my house, and I am entitled to be in my house!"

"Why aren't you at the pub?"

"Because I'm here. Are you OK, Louise? You seem angry."

"Why aren't you at the pub with Jackie, lips locked?"

James hadn't seen Louise like this before. She had sadness and anger in her eyes.

"What? You saw us?"

"Yes, I saw you." Louise threw her hands at James's chest, punching him as she shouted, "I saw you with Jackie! I saw you laughing! I saw you kissing!"

Tear started to roll down Louise's face, she couldn't help it. "I trusted you."

James held her back; she stopped punching him and held her head low.

James knew she was upset, she didn't hurt him when punching him but obviously he had hurt her.

"Why did you?"

"It isn't what you think. She came on to me. I just went for a quick drink. Would I have invited you if I wanted to be alone with her?

James lifted Louise's chin and stroked away the tears.

"I'm sorry. Really I am. I didn't mean to hurt you!"

"No, I'm sorry. I had no right to march round here and shout the odds."

"I'm glad you came."

"Are you?"

James gave Louise a peck on the cheek. The intense anger Louise had turned into intense passion. She stared up at him and felt her body melt as the ice blue eyes led her through to the main bedroom.

She started to undress him and her; thank God, she thought, she was wearing matching underwear.

The sexual tension and desire that had been building up between the two of them for ages was finally released.

James started to passionately kiss Louise. He was stroking her hair. His hand wandered, moving slowly down her slim neck, brushing across her breast. Louise's pleasure was audible.

Louise's hands began to wander over James's lean body, feeling every vein, bone and muscle.

He slowly and gently leaned in towards her and Louise felt a sudden rush of passionate desire. James breathlessly whispered, "I love you in more ways than you'll ever know. You're my girl, my world, my everything."

Louise giggled and replied, "This feels so right, I love you too."

Instead of the simple sex that couples have, all the emotion between the pair had resulting in making love.

It was so natural, so real. Louise had finally found a man she could trust. A man who didn't judge her because of her parents, because of her past, because of her personality, her image, her!

James too felt it was natural and real, he felt lucky to have caught Louise, lucky enough to have someone with a personality and a view on life.

James and Louise had spent the rest of the night curled up next to a fire, embraced in one another.

James looked at Louise; he looked deep into her eyes. Although there was a spark present, the mysterious look was still there!

James couldn't work it out, by trusting him, he thought that was why she looked so sad, because of trust.

The question to the eyes can't be love, it can't be trust, it can't be friendship! So what can it be? Why does her face tell one story and her eyes another? Which should I trust?

Chapter 14

LOUISE WAS PANICKING. WHAT HAD SHE done? Was it the right thing to do? It certainly felt right last night and early this morning when James had held her close, while watching her sleep. Louise had felt safe in the arms of a man and she had forgotten all her troubles. But surely she wouldn't be one of many one-night stands, would she?

James was in the shower; Louise made breakfast and had a bath.

They both decided to jog to work. This was a chance for Louise to think. As they jogged in silence, James was thinking, *Wow, that was fantastic last night. Nothing like I have ever experienced before, she was great and is great.*

Louise was thinking, *It was great, but was it a step too far too soon?*"

"Why are you smiling? You look like you are the cat who got the cream."

"That's because I am the cat who got the cream."

"And what cream is that, Mr Stewart?"

"That cream, Miss Adams, is you!"

Louise giggled. She was getting carried away again; it was the eyes that pulled her in like a magnet to metal. However, this attraction was stronger.

It seemed to Louise it was too good to be true. If Louise was true to herself, she would admit that although James was the best thing to be in her life, she found it hard to commit herself fully to him, just in case....

Hidden within her was a worry, a worry that increased with every hour of knowing James, increased when spending time in his company, when learning something new about him or when listening to him.

This had scared Louise, scared her that she was so insecure, that she couldn't or was it she wouldn't trust anyone?

She blamed her mother's words for this. When she was arguing with her father, she had said to Louise: "Never trust anyone, because if you do, you will only get hurt."

"You OK, Louise? You are crying!"

James stopped and turned to Louise. "Am I?"

Louise hadn't realised she had let the past catch up with her once again.

"It must be the wind."

James knew this was not the truth, but let it go.

They arrived at work together, and at once people began to talk. *Isn't that typical?* James thought that nothing in the world could be kept to oneself. *Your news is everyone else's.*

Everyone was happy for them. Sarah had whispered to Louise when James wasn't there, "He's the lucky one. Remember that."

Louise smiled. "Thanks, Sarah."

To come to think about it everyone was happy and supportive of the newfound love, apart from Jackie.

Now that was no surprise there. James hadn't forgotten about Monday night in the pub. In one way he was glad Louise saw them because that was what made her come round his. However, in many other ways, James wasn't glad and he let Jackie know just how he felt.

"Just to let you know, I was not interested. I am not interested and I never will be interested!"

Jackie gave James a look of spite. Out of every man she had ever laid her eyes on, James was the one she had out everything in to capturing, but she hadn't succeeded. Louise would pay for this; she just didn't know it yet!

The day went quickly and Louise found hardly any time at all to think, the buzz in her life was magical. She felt alive and she felt happy to be where she was today.

At the end of the day, all Louise was looking forward to was a quiet night in.

At six o'clock she was just finishing her typing, the office was empty apart from Jackie. Why would Jackie still be working? She was a 9-to-5 girl and nothing more.

She was just sitting there, waiting. Louise grabbed her bag, stood up and as she did, Jackie stood up.

"Louise, I just wanted to say I'm happy for you and James. I'm happy that you have found someone. Although he is only after one thing and I'm sorry to say you're not the girl to give him that. Look closer to home."

The same smirk appeared on her face as she walked out.

Chapter 15

LOUISE'S ANGER WAS VANISHING. AT FIRST the words that came out of Jackie's mouth had hit her, hit her right in the heart.

It took her awhile to understand the meaning behind the words "He is only after one thing." Well, as far as Louise could figure, he had achieved that. "Look closer to home." Closer to home, my family, friends—no what Jackie meant, and Louise knew, was her!

Well, she was wrong. If James was only after one thing, how come he was still around? And if Jackie was the girl for him, why hadn't he made a move?

Louise arrived home, and spent time with Sophie. She didn't feel hungry. She climbed into bed early that night with her favourite novel and an extra quilt.

The rest of the week, Louise and James spent a lot of time together. Sunday was a lazy day and Louise went to bed early again.

When waking early the next morning, Louise was feeling very ill; all the muscles in her back had tightened. She wasn't hungry.

Sophie knew this was so, although Sophie came to Louise as a pup and you would have thought that she would have been trained and knew Louise well. It was amazing to see how she would try and comfort her owner. She jumped onto her lap and flattered her ears. Louise stroked Sophie and when mentioned about a walk, Sophie jumped with excitement.

Louise jogged around Hyde Park twice, only stopping to be sick at the end of her gate. *Served me right for not eating then running*, Louise thought.

Louise looked at her watch; she had an hour to get ready for work. She decided to grab a coffee on the way to work.

When entering the office, James was waiting to greet her.

"How are you, my princess?"

"I'm OK, you?"

"I'm good, thank you. I have a couple of large cases to complete then I'm all yours."

Louise looked at James. The same ice blue eyes were present, the ones that had first caught her attention. Was he too good to be true? she wondered. Was there some hidden fault?

Louise shook these thoughts out of her head. James looked at Louise; the mysterious eyes were still there and this made him smile; he would have to work on them. He would have to figure the message out, but not yet and not today; he was too busy.

Louise splashed water over her face. That was the second time in the space of the morning she had been sick.

She made her excuses and went to the doctor's, James offered to go with her but she told him there was no need and that she would ring him later in the day.

Jackie caught Louise as she was leaving the office. "Isn't your puppy following?"

"You're only jealous, because you haven't got him."

"Maybe you're right. I haven't got him but I can and I will get him, and thanks to your nervous system, I have the rest of the afternoon to work on it!"

Louise had never hated anyone in her life and would do anything for anyone but Jackie was testing that quality of hers.

"Good morning, what can I get for you?"

"I'm not sure really, a cup of tea would be nice."

"I meant health wise."

Louise blushed, she was never good at discussing problems. "I feel sick."

"How long have you felt?"

"From last week. It's probably a tummy bug."

"A tummy bug, I doubt it, Miss Adams. I wonder if you would mind if I examined you."

Louise stripped her clothes off, the doctor examined her, she dressed and sat down.

"Well, you certainly keep yourself in shape; I suppose you will find that harder now!"

"Why?"

"Because you're pregnant, Miss Adams. Congratulations."

Chapter 16

LOUISE COULDN'T BREATHE. SHE GASPED FOR air. "Are you OK, Miss Adams? Are you not feeling too well?"

Louise stood up and blacked out.

When she woke, she was being comforted by the doctor. He had a warm smile, and a gentle voice, a father figure. He cooled her head with a towel and handed her a cup of tea.

"But I can't be pregnant."

"You are."

"But I can't, I'm not ready. I haven't had experience of the world yet. I'm not married, I'm not even engaged, it's all wrong! It's not supposed to be like this."

"Calm down, Miss Adams, it will be OK."

After Louise had drunk her cup of tea, she had made steady progress to the exit and made her way home.

She rang work and booked two days off for sickness. She decided to walk home. Her whole body felt heavy. She dragged her feet along the ground.

When passing Hyde Park and seeing little children running

around, she felt sick. She wasn't ready to have a child; it would be unfair on the child. Tears started to roll down her cheek. Being pregnant was supposed to be a happy time. You were the creator of a life. Louise couldn't face this responsibility!

She dreamed of a white wedding, a year spent together, and when the foundations were laid then children. Instead, there were no foundations but the bearing of a child.

Louise returned soaked through by her tears, she didn't even bother to undress, she pulled a duvet out of the cupboard and curled up in bed.

She slept for a number of hours; the emotions displayed earlier on in the day had worn her out.

It was against Louise's morals to get rid of God's creation and so the only other option was to keep the child. While asleep the motto that her father once told her kept circling around her mind: "No one can make you feel inferior unless you give them the consent to do so!"

She agreed; however, she felt ashamed and embarrassed. She felt insecure and worried about people's reactions.

While she was worrying about how she was to cope, she forgot about James. He had to know, didn't he?

Well, he was the father; Louise could predetermine what his reaction would be. He wouldn't want to be with her, he wouldn't want to talk to her let alone see her.

She had made him out to be a fool; an uncontrolled night of passion had led to an uncontrolled pregnancy.

Louise rang James. He had the right to know and the way she was feeling at the moment allowed her to ring him. She couldn't be made more upset and if she did it wouldn't have mattered.

She prepared herself for the worst, a skill her mother had taught her.

"Hello."

"Hi, Louise. How are you feeling? Do you need anything? I can always come over and give you some TLC!" James giggled.

How could Louise tell him, especially over the phone? She would have to tell him face to face, but not at work.

"James, I'm sorry. How will you ever forgive me?"

"Why are you saying sorry? Don't tell me you have killed the flowers I bought for you. You're too apologetic, Lou."

Louise burst into tears; he had no idea, and the guilt was unbearable.

"What's wrong, Louise? I can always buy you some more flowers."

"It's not that it's…"

Louise couldn't bring herself to say it. She put the phone down and slid down the kitchen door.

Twenty minutes later, James had left work, made some excuse about needing to work at home and drove to Louise's. There was no answer at the door so he decided to high jump over the gate, only succeeding with the third try. When over the gate, Sophie was jumping up and managed to open the gate with her paws.

James blushed. How obvious to press the handle down; instead, he was acting like a fake Jackie Chan. He shook himself and remembered why he was there. He ran to the back, opened the back door and found Louise in floods of tears.

She looked so fragile and doll-like. James comforted her. He carried her to the cream sofa and made her a cup of tea.

"What's wrong? Who or what has made you so upset?"

"I am so sorry, James. I didn't mean to."

"Mean to what?"

"I'm pregnant."

Louise lowered her head. He lifted her chin, looked into her eyes and said, "That's the best piece of news I have heard all day, apart from West Ham winning 2-0," he laughed.

"You're not angry? Upset? Ashamed?"

"Of course not. I told you, you're my love, my girl, my world, my everything. I will be there for you."

Louise believed what he said was the truth!

Chapter 17

THE COLOUR RETURNED TO LOUISE'S FACE. This morning sickness routine was becoming tedious.

James and Louise decided to keep the news to themselves for a while. Plans needed to be made, and it was just them that would be making them!

James spent the rest of the two days with Louise. Between working he would make her cups of tea and bring her raisins, grapes, apples and bread.

This had made him laugh. Louise still was eating for one, if you could call eating fruit for one. James would tease her about this but Louise would reassure him she was OK.

Later on Louise had turned to James; she was planning to go back to work. James appreciated this and it made him feel relieved in a way that he would be able to keep an eye on her.

Louise turned up to work with a radiant glow. She was wearing a black suit, bought by James as a gift to celebrate. He had made an oath to stick by her. So when Louise saw him that morning, she smiled. While sitting there working, she glanced up to see the blue eyes. Every now and then they would catch each other's eyes.

Louise giggled and emailed James.

From: Louise
To: James

I feel like a teenager hiding a secret from the rest of the world! "I know something you don't know!"

From: James
To: Louise

This secret won't be a secret for long. "No one in the world has secrets." Someone someway always knows what it is you're hiding. The truth will always come out.

Louise sat there and reread the email. He was right; however, she felt guilty not telling her parents but then guilt was a wasted emotion!

From: Louise
To: James

Not just a pretty face.

James knew that Louise had a secret she wasn't sharing; it was shown in her eyes. Louise carried on working. She had gained energy from somewhere and would have kept working if she wasn't interrupted by an email.

She looked up and over at James's desk. He was not there, so it wasn't from him.

From: Mike
To: Louise

Hi Louise,
Hope you are feeling better! It has come to our attention as management that a problem has occurred. You are not to worry at all, but it would be nice if these questions had answers. I have arranged a meeting at 2 with myself and Dave, if you could attend that would be great.

Many thanks,
Mike
X

Louise's mind was racing: *What questions? What answers?* She had only been off for two days. She grabbed a quick lunch, smartened her appearance up and left a note for James.

Mike and Dave were on floor one. A big conference room was full of coffee and tea, this was the head office of the criminal law department.

Louise made her was down to 101. This was the worst feeling in the world not knowing the unexpected.

Louise didn't like confrontations; she never had. She would either giggle or fiddle with her hair. Even if she knew she was in the right, she would never say so. You could say although her body was of a twenty-four-year-old, her emotional mind wasn't. This was her fault in life.

Louise took a deep breath, straightened up and knocked twice on the glass door.

"Good afternoon, Louise. Please sit down."

Mike and Dave were both in the room. Louise was and felt outnumbered. *This can't be good*, she thought.

"I hope you are OK. I would just like to say how we have noticed how efficient—"

"Don't ramble on, Mike. Just get to the point!"

Mike continued, "We have been informed that you are expecting."

How did he know that, not James? He wouldn't; he promised!

"Yes, I am."

"Well, our company policy states that we can not, under any circumstances, keep you on! When you have had your child, maybe then we can consider an opportunity if your vacancy hasn't been filled."

"I don't understand."

"I'm sorry to let you go. I wish you every success."

Louise was dumbfounded. Surely this was discrimination; she had been discriminated.

Chapter 18

MIKE CARRIED ON TO MAKE HIS apologises and gave her till the end of the week to leave. Dave, the arrogant bastard, never said a word and left giving Louise a disgusted look.

Louise began to walk out the door until a sudden burst of frustration filled her. She turned around and said, "Mike, I was just wondering, who told you?"

Mike didn't look up; the name flew out of his mouth, the name that made Louise see red—the name was Jackie. Why was this person put on the earth to destroy her ambitions?

Louise walked along the corridor with her head held high, she turned the corner and into the lift.

Well, the phrase was, bad luck comes in threes!

Louise got to her office, neatly packed her belongings and went home without saying a word to anyone.

When arriving at home, she decided to ring her sister and brother. Vicky, as Louise knew, hit the night life 360 days a year, the other five were recovery days.

She picked up the phone and prayed her sister was in.

"Hello."

"Hi, sis."

"Oh, hi, how are you? I was getting ready to go out!"

"What at three in the afternoon." Louise giggled.

"Well, you know I have to be groomed."

"Of course, so any news?"

"Apart from I happened to get an audition for the musicals *Chicago* and *We Will Rock* you as a dancer, nothing much."

"Oh, that's fantastic! I'm really pleased, so you are a champion."

"Eh?"

"You know, the song 'We Are the Champions.'"

Oh no that started Vicky off.

"Sorry, sis, anyway how are you?"

"I'm OK, I have some news."

"Don't tell me you and James are getting married."

"No."

"You haven't broken up, have you?"

"No, no. It's worse than that. I'm pregnant."

"Well, that's fantastic. Actually, Lou, couldn't you have waited a couple more years? I mean I'm going to be an aunt, and I really am not old enough to be one yet. Yet, actually, maybe it is a good thing. I will be able to play on it. Auntie Vicky—it's got a ring to it, don't you think?"

"I also lost my job."

"Ah, well, that's not good news, erm, you could always work for me as my tour manager!"

"Thanks, Vicky."

"So you're pleased?"

"Yes, thanks."

"Lou, just to say I will support you, whatever happens."

"Thanks."

"I mean that. I know I have been a cow in the past, but I'll be there."

Louise said all she had to say and let her sister go off and get ready.

Next Louise was to ring her brother; hopefully he would be back from football.

"Hello."

"Hi, Luke."

"Hi, mate, you OK? I've just got in, 3-0. I scored two."

"Well done! I'm good thanks. I thought I would ring you to let you know I'm pregnant and I have lost my job."

Every time Louise said it, it became easier!

"Is that what you want?"

"To lose my job? No. But to be pregnant, I don't know."

"All women are the same. You're just like Jen, and I bet you're just eating for one."

"Luke, stop. Who's Jen?"

"You know the bean pole I took to Mum's party? Well, she won't be a bean pole for long!"

"Oh, my God. No!"

"Yes."

"I'm so happy for you, Luke. When did you find out?"

"Today, well about four minutes ago. You're the first person I have told."

"Ah, thanks."

"We will get through this together. I can't believe I'm going to be a father and an uncle. They are both going to be West Ham supporters, OK?"

Louise giggled. "How do you know they are going to be both boys?"

"OK, well, if it's a girl, she can be a cheerleader!"

"OK, deal."

"OK, sweetie, well you look after yourself and I will get Jen to come round one night and James can come round mine. Until then, take care!"

A warm glow lay in Louise's stomach, she felt for once her brother and sister would be there to support her and not judge her!

Chapter 19

JAMES HAD TURNED UP HALF AN hour ago, Louise had explained all about work, about Dave and Mike.

James was livid. "They can't do that, that's against the law, isn't it?"

Louise then explained about Jackie and how Mike said she was the one who told him.

James looked at Louise. "So?"

"So, James, Jackie has had it in for me since day one. She tried to get with you twice or even three times, then she gets me the sack."

"No, Louise, you have had it in for Jackie since day one. You judged her the minute you saw her, because of her appearance!"

"What?"

"I could have had her if I wanted her and you know it, you were a challenge!"

"Excuse me. I knew it. She was right. You were only after one thing. How could I have been so naive?"

"I didn't mean that, Louise. I'm sorry. I'm just a bit stressed out with work at the moment."

"I knew it. I have tried so hard not to become a statistic, to not become like my parents. I personally thought I had succeeded. Obviously not. You're just like the rest of them."

"Them?"

"Yes, men! When I thought Jackie had got you, that was one door closed, then I was looking for another door opening, but I looked so regretfully upon the door that was closed, that I didn't see the ones opening for me. Instead, I came round yours. I should have gone then, I should have left you with Jackie in the pub."

"What are you saying, Lou?"

"I'm saying it's over."

"You don't know what you are talking about. It's your emotions; they are playing up."

"No, they are not. I'm in control of my emotions. You are the one who needs controlling."

James left. He held his head low, so there was no sight of his blue eyes. He walked to the gate, got into his car and fell forward. It looked to Louise as though he was crying. She had never seen him cry before and she didn't like it.

Louise fell onto the sofa. She began to cry. She couldn't do anything else but cry. The man who had told her she was his love, his princess, his life and his everything was gone! The man who was the father of he child had left. The man who made her feel alive had left. The man who she trusted had left.

Louise looked out the window; the car had gone. The man who owned the Focus had left.

Louise froze. If this man had really gone, she would never see the blue eyes again. The eyes that, as her mother put it, were come-to-bed eyes. The eyes that had first attracted Louise had disappeared.

Chapter 20

"IT'S AN UNDOUBTED TRUTH, LOUISE, THAT the less one has to do, the less time one finds to do it."

"You have to kiss an awful lot of frogs, before you get a prince."

That was referring to her own love life, Louise had met up with Matt and her mum for lunch.

"Sorry, dear, I was getting carried away with my own love life."

"Louise, look at everything as though you were seeing it either for the first or last time. Then your time on earth will be filled glory."

Louise looked at her mother although she was her mother she was wise.

"People don't seem to realise how often you have to come in second in order to finish first. I've never met a winner who hadn't learned how to be a loser. And with you and James well 'To forgive is human to forget is divine.' Louise, I hope you can forgive me for all that has happened in the past. I didn't mean to hurt you."

Louise gave her mum a hug, then Matt. She was happy to see her mother happy, and what she had said was thought-provoking.

Louise decided to meet up with James soon she promised.

As Louise finished her lunch, she said her goodbyes and went to go home. As she reached the restaurant door, her mother shouted: "Louise, remember this if nothing else. Nothing in life is to be feared. It is only to be understood."

Chapter 21

HER MOTHER WAS CONSTANTLY WITH MATT and her father with Holly. They were both pleased for her, especially her father. He had been over the moon. To celebrate, he took her out on her own to a candlelight dinner. This really made Louise happy. In the past twenty-four years, she hadn't ever been alone with her father.

She spent the evening forgetting all her troubles. For a while she forgot she was pregnant, until the child kicked.

She had felt special, her dad talked for hours about Holly, what she liked, disliked, etc.

Louise knew he was happy and she hoped she would be too.

As the evening drew to a close, Louise and her father decided to take a walk along the river. They walked in silence for a while.

"I had a phone call from James this morning."

"Did you?"

"Yes, he sounded distraught. What did you say to him? He was like a man who had no life in him."

"I was out of order. I said things I didn't mean to say. I was upset."

"That is no excuse, Louise, and you know that."

Louise knew her father was right. He handed her his phone and said, "Do the right thing."

Louise rang James and apologised. Her father was proud of her for ringing him and said, "I know that was hard. Well done. I love you, Louise, don't forget it."

The blue eyes reappeared at Louise's front door eight o'clock Sunday morning. Louise was taking Sophie out for a walk. She couldn't speak; she felt so ashamed about her actions the other night. She couldn't look at James in the eye, so she decided to listen to what he had to say.

"Louise, I'm sorry about what I said the other night. I never want Jackie. You are the only one I want."

"That's OK. I was out of order too. Let's forget about it!"

"OK."

They spent the rest of the day together, discussing plans for the baby, and about the situation about work.

It felt normal to be together, to be arm in arm just the two of them. Actually it was now the three of them!

Chapter 22

LOUISE WAS EIGHT AND A HALF months pregnant. As she was reading another book, Louise had her mind wandering; thoughts about her plan to become an independent solicitor where James would be her partner. The idea when mentioned made Louise's heart race. It was so exciting planning the unexpected.

She had met up with Jen, earlier in the week. Behind the naive model life of hers, she turned out to be a lovely girl. She helped Louise figure out names, etc.

Louise couldn't believe how relaxed Jen was. She was also glad to hear that Luke was looking after her well. She seemed to thrive on the attention.

Louise was interrupted, the phone rang: "Hello."

"Hi, Lou. It's me."

"Hi, James. You OK—?"

"Wait before you go on, I can't do this anymore. I'm sorry. I just can't. I have tried since the first time I fell in love with you, the first time my eyes met yours. Louise, I'm sorry. I find it too hard. I can't cope. I hope you won't mind. It's just me rushing back every night to see you then going home to then come back in the morning."

"I understand, James."

"No, I don't think you do. I'm sorry."

He hung up, Louise couldn't believe it, she was due to have her child it two weeks and now she would really be a statistic. All the hard work ruined.

She held her stomach and felt her child kick. She prayed that her child would find a man or woman one day who would look after him or her.

Sophie started to bark. "Sophie." Louise went to pull her away from the window but she wouldn't budge.

The doorbell rung, Louise opened the door. Before her was James. Her eyes must have been misleading her. For there, in the flesh, James bent on one knee, with six yellow, white, pink and now red roses in one hand; in the other hand was a box.

"But on the phone, you said sorry, I thought that meant it was over."

"It does. I meant I can't go on living separate lives. We have a child on the way and our whole lives to live. Louise?"

"Yes."

James stared on the floor, his blue eyes sparkled. "Will you make me the happiest man alive?"

"What?"

"Will you take the roses?"

"Yes."

"And would you take the box, put the ring on and say yes?"

"Are you asking me to marry you?"

"Yes, I am, Miss Adams, soon-to-be Mrs Stewart."

Louise flew her arms around James, nearly knocking him over with her weight, and kissed him.

The ring was elegant, small and just right.

"Don't worry about anything. When one loves somebody, everything is clear—where to go, what to do, it all takes care of itself—and one doesn't have to ask anybody about anything."

Louise looked at James. He was serious. She felt so happy. James helped Louise back into the flat. They made dinner and watched some TV.

It was twelve o'clock. Louise was in a lot of pain. James had popped out to collect the rest of his work. He finished work on Friday and needed to finish some cases off.

Louise held her stomach. The sharp pains were becoming more regular and Louise feared the worst.

She looked at the note on the roses: "Where there is great love, there are miracles!"

Chapter 23

LOUISE'S WATERS HAD BROKEN. THIS WAS it. This was the day, the time now! She remained calm; she rang James who grabbed all of her essentials, including Sophie and drove her to Mayflower hospital.

Once they arrived, Louise was rushed off to the operating room. All Louise could think about was: *Please don't let me have a caesarean.* The nurse found this amusing, considering the amount of pain the patient was experiencing.

James was by Louise's side the whole way through. "Don't leave me. Please don't leave me."

"I won't, I'm here and always will be."

James gave her a wink, her heart did a somersault.

3:20, that was when the miracle happened. The miracle was called Annabel. She weighed 6 pounds 10 ounces and was gorgeous.

"She has your nose."

"She has your hair."

"She has your smile."

Louise looked at Annabel; she opened her mouth and giggled.

James rolled his eyes. "I will never hide from that giggle."

Louise looked at her own flesh and blood. She froze; the child's eyes opened and an identical pair of deep ice blue eyes like James's stared back at her. What a lovely gift to have a pair of eyes like that.

James looked at Louise. Their eyes were locked for a moment, but within the moment James had noticed the mysterious eyes that had once attracted him to her had disappeared and vanished!

However, James had noticed another attraction; her deep brown eyes were full of happiness.

"Louise, what happened to your eyes?"

"It just clicked."

"What has?"

"James, will you do me a big favour?"

"Of course."

Louise put Annabel down to sleep. "Would you listen to what I have to say?"

"Yes."

"It's just clicked. All my life, I have lived to not be a statistic, lived to not fall into groupings, to not be stereotyped. I made this decision when my parents got divorced. Although they are happy now, I didn't want that to happen to me. However, being a statistic is living. We are all statistics. You live, you die, if you like it or not, you are at the end of the day a number in a big book. I thought it was wrong to be divorced, be with a child with no father or not married. To be sacked or to have an illness. That's why I also hide my emotions or try to."

She giggled, tears were rolling down her face. "I try to hide the fact that my parents were divorced, then when you told me your parents were divorced, I felt ashamed that I could have judged you. I had made it my ambition in life to not be a percentage of the world. So when we first met, I thought you would help me with my goal. I could trust you. When I saw you with Jackie at the pub my heart broke in two. The pain I felt was unbearable."

James walked over to the bed and held her hand, his ice blue eyes were shedding tears. This picture of the two of them crying and Annabel laughing was picture perfect.

"I suddenly felt that I hadn't tried hard enough to not be a statistic, I felt like a one-night stand. Then I became pregnant. I felt ashamed. Another stereotyped woman who was not married but yet pregnant. Then bad luck comes in threes and I got the sack, another statistic. It felt as though I was taking a step forward. I was really taking three steps back. The harder I tried to avoid being a statistic, the more I was becoming one. So as I look at our child, I've clicked that no one can hide from being a statistic. It's not possible. Although I live every day to the fullest, I don't have to follow routines. I am who I am and I have to accept that and so does everyone else."

Louise stopped and she looked at James. Her heart lit up. She had realised at that moment in time that she was the luckiest girl alive.

"I didn't know you felt like that."

"You do now." Louise giggled. Her smile was amazing. She was radiant and glowing with life.

"I would just like to say, Louise, and I have said it in the past. You are my love, my girl, my princess, my everything and that is still true but…"

Louise's smile faded. "What?"

"You will have to share me and my blue eyes with Annabel now!"

Printed in the United States
46115LVS00006B/103-153